The Karate Kid Part III

The
Karate Kid
Part III

COLUMBIA PICTURES Presents A JERRY WEINTRAUB Production   A Film By JOHN G. AVILDSEN
"THE KARATE KID PART III" Starring RALPH MACCHIO   NORIYUKI "PAT" MORITA
MUSIC BY BILL CONTI MUSIC SUPERVISOR BROOKS ARTHUR EXECUTIVE PRODUCER SHELDON SCHRAGER
CO-PRODUCER KAREN TRUDY ROSENFELT WRITTEN BY ROBERT MARK KAMEN BASED ON CHARACTERS CREATED BY ROBERT MARK KAMEN
PRODUCED BY JERRY WEINTRAUB DIRECTED BY JOHN G. AVILDSEN

The Karate Kid Part III

A novelization for young readers by B. B. Hiller.
Based on a motion picture written by Robert Mark Kamen.
Based on characters created by Robert Mark Kamen.

SCHOLASTIC INC.
New York Toronto London Auckland Sydney

ISBN 0-590-43042-4

12 11 10 9 8 7 6 5 4 3 2   9/8 0 1 2 3/9

Printed in the U.S.A.   11

First Scholastic printing, July 1989

*This book is dedicated to
Andrew Neil Hiller*

The Karate Kid Part III

1

It seemed to Daniel LaRusso that everything was changing all at once.

He'd just come back home to California from Okinawa, where he had spent the summer with his friend, Mr. Miyagi. But when Daniel got home he found that his home was gone. The apartment building he lived in was being torn down. That meant that Mr. Miyagi was out of a job, too, since he worked at the building. And Daniel found out that his mother had flown to New Jersey to take care of a sick uncle. She had arranged to have Daniel stay in California with Mr. Miyagi so he could start college the following week.

There was an awful lot to do before that happened. First, Daniel and Mr. Miyagi had to move all of Mr. Miyagi's belongings out of his workroom at the apartment building before the wreckers got to it. Mr. Miyagi had been the handyman at the

1

building for a long time. He had a lot of tools there. He also kept bonsai trees there.

Mr. Miyagi loved bonsai. He also loved karate. He'd taught Daniel a lot about karate and a little bit about bonsai. Bonsai were miniature trees. They never grew to more than about ten inches, even if they were a hundred years old. Mr. Miyagi had shown Daniel how to clip the branches of a sapling to make it become a bonsai. Mr. Miyagi had done it thousands of times. He had a big collection of trees. Daniel helped him put them in the truck to take to Mr. Miyagi's house.

Daniel felt sad for Mr. Miyagi. Although Mr. Miyagi was old enough to retire, it was hard for Daniel to think of him not working. Also, Daniel knew that Mr. Miyagi didn't have much money saved. Not only would he want to have another job, he'd *have* to get one.

"Hey, Mr. Miyagi," Daniel said, climbing into the front of the truck with his friend when they were done loading it. "Did you ever think about opening a bonsai store?"

"In my dreams, Daniel-san," he said. "In my retirement." In Japanese, it was polite to add "-san" to the end of a person's name. It showed respect, the way Daniel showed his friend respect by calling him *Mr.* Miyagi. Daniel didn't even know Mr. Miyagi's first name.

"Well, what do you call this?" Daniel asked.

"Call it time to go," Mr. Miyagi said. He had a funny way of changing the subject when his mind was made up about something. Mr. Miyagi turned on the engine in his truck and headed for home.

Daniel wasn't ready to stop thinking about the bonsai shop, though. As they drove, he worked on the problem. The problem, of course, was money. Daniel thought there might be a way around it.

"Hey, Mr. Miyagi, I've been thinking about the bonsai shop," Daniel said later, when they were unloading the truck at Mr. Miyagi's house. "You already have all the trees you need to open a shop." He pointed to the truckload of miniature trees. "How hard could it be?"

"Probably not very, if I had money to rent shop and renovate it. But no have money, Daniel-san."

"Yes, you do," Daniel said. He reached into his pocket and pulled out all of his money. It was the money he was supposed to spend on college, but Mr. Miyagi was his best friend, and Daniel thought he needed the money more than Daniel did.

"Thank you, Daniel-san, but that is not money," Mr. Miyagi said.

Daniel examined the money. He sniffed at it. "Looks like money to me. Smells like money."

"Smells like college education to me."

"Maybe, but I've got an idea," Daniel said.

"No ideas. Discussion is closed."

That's what Mr. Miyagi thought. When Daniel got an idea into his head, it could be hard to get it out. Daniel thought this was one of those times.

2

Daniel had a surprise gift for Mr. Miyagi. It was the most grown-up thing Daniel had ever done. He was excited. He hoped his friend would be, too.

"Mr. Miyagi, I'm home," Daniel called from the doorway. He could smell something good cooking in the kitchen. He went in there.

"How was first day of college?" Mr. Miyagi asked.

"Uh, I didn't go to college," Daniel said.

Mr. Miyagi looked at him coldly. "What?" he asked.

Now was time for the surprise. Daniel handed Mr. Miyagi his gift. It was enclosed in a black lacquer box and looked very formal. "May all your dreams come true," Daniel said.

"What's this?" Mr. Miyagi asked, taking the box.

"Only one way to find out."

Mr. Miyagi opened the box and took out the paper that was inside. "A lease? With my name on it? What did I rent?"

"It's your new bonsai store," Daniel said. Then he added, "Congratulations. And we even have enough money left over to fix up the place!"

Daniel could tell that Mr. Miyagi was very pleased, but he was also concerned. "You used your college money for this, Daniel-san. I can't have you do that!"

Daniel was going to have to be very persuasive. "Look," he said. "I'm going to take the year off, work in the shop, and help you make a success of it. See, I've been going to school non-stop since I was five. I could use a break."

Mr. Miyagi looked dubious.

"Come on, let me show you the place," Daniel said.

Mr. Miyagi turned off the stove and followed Daniel to his car. They drove to the downtown area of the town where they lived, Reseda. Daniel turned off the main street. He certainly hadn't had enough money to rent one of those shops! He made two more turns and then crossed the railroad tracks. There was the shop.

"The landlord said the neighborhood's up-and-coming," Daniel told Mr. Miyagi as they walked to the door. "Look, there's a pottery shop across the street. Maybe we can get some special planters made up for the trees. It's going to be great. Wait until you see inside."

Mr. Miyagi was quiet. Daniel could tell he was thinking. Daniel unlocked the door. The inside was a total mess. The shop had been a fruit packing plant. The floor was littered with parts of wooden crates.

"See all the wood; we can use it for our shelves and cabinets." Daniel pointed to a big crate. "And this can be a counter. Over there we can have our bonsai hospital. You know, in case any of the little guys get sick. I have a name for the shop, too. We can call it 'Mr. Miyagi's Little Trees.' Like it?"

Mr. Miyagi walked all around the shop, studying it. Then, after a few minutes he pulled the lease out of his pocket and studied that, too.

Daniel was getting nervous about the long silence. "Did I forget something?" he asked.

"*Hai*. You forgot to put your name on lease, next to mine, partner."

7

Daniel could hardly believe it. Not only did Mr. Miyagi agree to opening the shop and letting Daniel wait to start school, but he even wanted to be partners. If everything was changing all at once, at least it was changing for the better.

3

Not only did Daniel and Mr. Miyagi have to do a lot of work to fix up the shop, they also needed to collect some new trees to make into bonsai. They took a camping trip to a nearby forest to see if they could find any likely candidates. It turned out that the forest was full of saplings that were just the right size.

"This is a good one," Mr. Miyagi said. "Make special bonsai."

Daniel looked at the scrawny little sapling. "You really see a bonsai here?" he asked.

"*Hai*. Look inside," Mr. Miyagi answered. Then, very carefully, he dug out around the sapling, taking all of its roots. He packed the root ball in a plastic bag and gave the little tree to Daniel to carry.

"I don't get it," Daniel said.

"Look inside you," Mr. Miyagi explained. "Same place your karate comes from."

"But my karate comes from you," Daniel said.

"Only root of your karate comes from me. Like true bonsai, choose own way to grow. Because root is strong. You choose own way to do karate same reason."

"But I do it your way."

"And one day you will do it own way," Mr. Miyagi said.

Daniel thought about what his teacher — or *sensei*, as the word was in Japanese — had said. He thought it meant that Mr. Miyagi was teaching him only the roots of karate and that his karate would grow from those roots in the way that he would decide. It sounded very complicated, especially since everything he knew about karate, every move, every technique, had come straight from Mr. Miyagi. Those weren't roots; that was a whole tree!

They walked through the woods. Mr. Miyagi gave Daniel more of an explanation. "True karate like true bonsai," he said. "If strong root, tree is free to choose own best way to grow. Same karate. Miyagi give you strong root. You free to choose own way to grow."

"But bonsai aren't free to choose. We tell them how to grow with our clippers."

"Our bonsai not true bonsai. True bonsai grow wild. Only nature tell how to grow. True bonsai, natural bonsai, very rare."

Daniel had never heard of such a thing. "Ever see any?"

"In Okinawa," Mr. Miyagi said. That was where Mr. Miyagi had been born. "Brought to America with me. One natural bonsai from cliff on sea, north side of Okinawa. Remind me of home."

"Where's the bonsai now?"

"There," Mr. Miyagi said, pointing through the woods. "In Devil's Cauldron. In lovely, safe place."

Devil's Cauldron was a remote part of the Pacific coast. It was a tall cliff going down to the ocean around a cove. The whole thing was shaped like a deep teacup or a cauldron.

"Why'd you put it there?" Daniel asked.

"When Miyagi go fight in World War II, no one to take care of tree if something happen to me. Figure best was to put tree where tree take care of self. Back in nature."

"There are a lot of places in nature easier to get to," Daniel said.

11

"Daniel-san, know how much collector pay for original bonsai? Thousands of dollars! Better tree live where no one can see."

"But you can't see it, either," Daniel reminded him.

Then Mr. Miyagi told Daniel he could see it in his mind and in his heart, and that was enough for him.

Daniel shook his head. He couldn't imagine putting something precious on a cliff. He also couldn't imagine putting something beautiful out of sight. What could have made Mr. Miyagi think the tree was safer there than with an owner to take care of it? Mr. Miyagi had a way of looking at things that didn't always make sense to Daniel, but he usually found that it made sense to Mr. Miyagi, and that was good enough for Daniel.

4

A few days later Daniel pulled the morning's mail out of the mailbox. He flipped through the letters. One was for Mr. Miyagi from the All-Valley Tournament. That was the karate tournament Daniel had entered a year ago and won. He'd become the champion by beating a boy named Johnny. Johnny's *sensei*, Kreese, had wanted to win at all costs. He had been so angry about losing that he had attacked Mr. Miyagi after the tournament. Mr. Miyagi had beaten Kreese easily and embarrassed him, too. All of Kreese's students had dropped out of his *dojo*, Cobra Kai. They didn't want to study with someone who taught that you could only win when you cheated.

Daniel held the envelope up to the light. He couldn't see what it was. He took it to Mr. Miyagi.

Mr. Miyagi was sitting in his garden shed in

front of one of the saplings they'd collected in the forest. Daniel watched for a moment. Mr. Miyagi did things differently from anybody else Daniel had ever known. He fascinated Daniel.

Mr. Miyagi looked at the sapling. Then he closed his eyes. Daniel thought Mr. Miyagi was trying to figure out what was "inside." He opened his eyes again. He scowled. Then he closed them again. His clippers were right next to his right hand, but Daniel knew he would not touch them until he found the tree "inside."

Daniel cleared his throat. Mr. Miyagi looked up at him and smiled. "Look what came in the mail," Daniel said. "I *think* it's the application from the All-Valley Tournament. It's almost time for me to defend my title."

"A mountain only has to be climbed one time, Daniel-san."

"But what if you like the view from the top?" Daniel asked. He could remember how good it had felt when he'd won the championship. Everybody in the crowd cheered for him. His mother cheered, his girlfriend cheered. Even Mr. Miyagi had cheered. Daniel had never been happier in his life. He wanted to have that feeling again.

"Come, we go work," Mr. Miyagi said.

Once again, Mr. Miyagi was changing the subject because he'd made up his mind. Daniel followed him as he walked through the house, out the front door, and climbed into his truck.

"I know you don't believe in fighting, Mr. Miyagi, but this isn't exactly fighting."

"Isn't exactly ballroom dancing," Mr. Miyagi said.

"What if I decide to fill out the application myself?"

Mr. Miyagi handed him a pen. Then, while Daniel stood in the driveway, Mr. Miyagi turned on the engine of his truck, shifted into gear, and drove away.

Daniel looked at the application and the pen. He didn't know what to do, so he decided to do nothing for a while. He had talked Mr. Miyagi into opening the bonsai shop; he could probably talk him into letting him enter the tournament. He folded the application, stuck it in his pocket, and prepared to drive to the shop himself. He could not resist the letter from the All-Valley Tournament. He opened it and read the contents. Just looking at the letter made him excited about the idea of winning again. He just *had* to convince Mr. Miyagi to change his mind. Then he had an idea of something Mr. Miyagi would like. Maybe it would help Mr. Miyagi change his mind. Daniel took the little sapling Mr. Miyagi had been working on.

"Look what I brought," Daniel said, bringing the little tree into the shop. "I thought a change of scenery might help you get what's inside to be outside."

Mr. Miyagi smiled. "Very thoughtful of you, Daniel-san."

Daniel put the tree on the table in the work area of the shop. Mr. Miyagi sat down in front of it and began studying it again. Daniel took up the sandpaper Mr. Miyagi had been using on the cabinet and continued the work there.

"Uh, I hope you don't mind. I opened the letter from the tournament. There was a note with the application. Would you like to hear what it said?"

"Sure," Mr. Miyagi said.

"It says that the defending champion only has to fight the final match. See, I won't have to qualify this time. It cuts down the fights to just one. That's better than last year, isn't it?"

"*Hai.*"

"And let's face it. It's another year. I'm a lot more experienced. Right?"

"*Hai.*"

"So I should seriously reconsider all this. Right?"

"Wrong. Should seriously consider getting new pots for bonsai."

There he went again — changing the subject.

"I don't see what the big deal is," Daniel said. He was getting frustrated.

"Daniel-san, karate used to defend honor or life mean something. Karate used to defend plastic-and-metal trophy, mean nothing. Now you find good pots."

5

A bell tinkled as Daniel walked into the pottery shop. "Hello?" he called out.

"I'm almost finished," a girl said from the back of the shop. Daniel wanted to see what she was finishing. He walked back to look.

She was working at a potter's wheel. The wheel was a flat disk, which rotated rapidly. At first there was just a big lump of clay in the center of it. Then the girl moistened her hands and began transforming the clay into a vase by moving her hands up and down and guiding the clay into the shape she wanted. It was almost magical.

"Hey, neat!" Daniel said.

The girl smiled at him. She was pretty. Daniel smiled back. She finished forming the vase and then made a design on it with some of the tools from the rack in front of her. "What can I do for you?" she asked.

"I was looking for some planters for bonsai trees. We're opening the shop across the street."

"Oh, welcome to the neighborhood," she said. She stood up and removed the vase from the wheel. Being very careful, she carried it over to the rack to dry.

"I love bonsai, they're so perfect," she said.

"You should come over and take a look when we move our trees in. And you can meet my partner."

"I haven't even met *you* yet," she said. "I'm Jessica Andrews."

He told her his name. They shook hands.

While Jessica tidied up the clay from the wheel, Daniel looked around the shop a little. He saw a lot of very nice bowls, vases, and pots. He also saw a picture of Jessica. She was hanging by a rope over a cliff.

"Is that you?" he asked.

"Yes. I was rappeling down that mountain. I do it to get different clays for the pots. Like to come along sometime?"

Daniel thought he'd rather fight ten bullies at once than dangle over a cliff like that . . . unless he could be with Jessica.

"Yeah, sure," he lied.

Just then a delivery truck arrived, and Jessica had to tell the men where to put the cartons.

"So, what should we do about your plants?" she asked.

"I had this idea for planters with a bonsai on the side, sort of like a trademark. Think you could do that?"

"Sounds like a great idea," she said. "I'll give you a sample and you see if you like it." Daniel was sure he would like whatever Jessica did.

Before he left, he had one other idea he wanted to discuss with Jessica — a date. She seemed to like that idea, too. They agreed that Daniel would come pick her up that evening at seven.

Daniel practically floated back to the bonsai shop. When he got there, Mr. Miyagi was hard at work. He was clipping away at the sapling, transforming it into a bonsai.

"You found it," Daniel said, meaning Mr. Miyagi had discovered the image inside of him.

"Thanks to you," Mr. Miyagi said. "You find anything?"

"Yeah, a date." Daniel told him about Jessica. "So what should I do about this?" he asked, pulling the tournament application out of his pocket.

"Don't look Miyagi for answer, Daniel-san. Like bonsai live inside tree, answer live inside you."

"Inside me right now is just a lot of confusion," Daniel said. "I mean, I could put a pen to this and end up champion again."

"Or put a match to it and let confusion go up in smoke."

Daniel knew he still wasn't ready to make up his mind. He concentrated on the work he had to do at the shop — and on the date he'd have with Jessica that evening.

6

"Say, Mr. Miyagi," Daniel said, going up the steps to the house two at a time later that day. "Can I borrow one of your fancy shirts for tonight?"

"Wear one with the big orchids. Women cannot resist big orchids," Mr. Miyagi said.

Daniel raised an eyebrow. "Sounds like the voice of experience speaking," he teased.

"Used to be voice. Now just a whisper."

Daniel laughed. He went into Mr. Miyagi's room, found the shirt with the orchids, and took it to his room to change for his date with Jessica.

He'd had a good afternoon, working hard. He and Mr. Miyagi always seemed to work well together. Together, they'd almost finished the shop. It looked very different from the place he'd rented just ten days earlier. It was neat and clean and freshly painted. The shelves and counters just needed a few finishing touches. They'd be ready to open in a few days. Daniel had even had some advertising flyers printed up. Everything seemed to be working out — Mr. Miyagi's dream, the shop, even Jessica.

Now, if only he could figure out what to do about the tournament. . . .

Daniel heard Mr. Miyagi's truck leave. He was going back to the shop to work for a few more hours. Nothing ever seemed to be too much for Mr. Miyagi. He was the hardest worker Daniel had ever known. Daniel was proud to learn from him. He was proud to learn about carpentry, plumbing, electricity, bonsai, and karate. Mr. Miyagi knew a lot about all of those things, and Daniel was his student in all of them.

Daniel thought for a moment about what it meant to be a student. It didn't always mean doing everything exactly the same way his teacher did, but that was where his roots came from. And what did that mean to Daniel about entering the tournament? As he thought about it, he decided it meant that Mr. Miyagi's way of karate did not include tournaments unless it was a question of defense or of honor. Glory had nothing to do with it. Since that was what his *sensei* believed, how could he believe anything different?

There was the answer.

Mr. Miyagi's truck pulled back into the driveway.

"Forget something?" Daniel asked when his friend came into the house.

"*Hai*, forgot this," he said, taking a bonsai statue off of the mantle. "For shop. Bring luck."

"Let's hope it brings customers, too."

"You look nice, Daniel-san," Mr. Miyagi told him.

Daniel looked at himself in the mirror. "Yeah, thanks for the shirt," Daniel said. Then he drew a piece of paper from his pocket. "Here's one tournament application that won't see the light of day," he said.

"What are you doing?" Mr. Miyagi asked.

"Taking your advice," Daniel told him. He took a match and lit it. Then he held it to the application and tossed the burning paper into the fireplace.

"Good, Daniel-san. Save on Band-Aids."

Daniel smiled. "You kidding? They never landed a hand on me last year."

Mr. Miyagi raised one eyebrow. "Couple of feet, maybe. Elbow, I think. Knee, for sure."

Daniel laughed. Mr. Miyagi was right: He'd taken quite a beating last year. This year, he did not have to do that again. He was glad he'd made up his mind, and he knew he'd made the right decision.

7

The first thing Jessica said when she saw Daniel was, "Nice shirt." Mr. Miyagi would be pleased about that!

As they walked, Jessica told Daniel that she was planning to move. She had come from Ohio, and she would be going back there in a couple of weeks. Daniel was sorry about that. He liked Jessica a lot, but they agreed to be friends until it was time for her to go.

Daniel wanted her to meet Mr. Miyagi, so he offered to take her over to the shop, where his partner was finishing up for the night.

"You are about to meet the greatest guy. He's smart. He's funny. You got a problem; he's got an answer. He's like no one you've ever met. And he's my best friend."

Mr. Miyagi was preparing to leave the shop

when they arrived. He bowed politely to Jessica. Jessica bowed back to him.

"Welcome to shop," he said. "Like to see inside?"

"Sure. How's it going so far?" she asked.

"Never knew retirement would be such hard work." He gave the keys to Daniel and reminded him to lock up when they left.

Daniel liked showing off their work to Jessica. The shop looked so nice. He told her how much work Mr. Miyagi had done.

"Boy, this place is going to be neat," she said. "I liked Mr. Miyagi, but he sure doesn't look like the karate-teacher type."

"He doesn't act like it much, either. Half the time, when he teaches me stuff, I don't even know what's being taught. Like the vase you were making; you can make a whole karate lesson out of it."

"Come on," Jessica said. She sounded like she didn't believe him.

"I'll show you." Daniel pulled over two fruit crates and they sat facing one another. "Now, do that motion."

Jessica pretended to make a vase on a make-believe potter's wheel. Daniel showed her how, if she speeded up the motion, she could learn a blocking technique. She was more surprised than Daniel when she found herself winning the match!

The door to the shop flew open. Two people came in. One was a boy about Daniel's age. The other was an older man. He looked like a tough guy from a movie. He acted like it, too. "Can I join the party?" the tough guy asked.

"We're not open for business," Daniel said.

"We came for a different kind of business," he told Daniel.

Daniel could not imagine what they wanted. After all, there was nothing to steal in the shop yet. But he didn't like the looks of these guys, and he was uncomfortable with them.

"We heard you're not entering the All-Valley this year," the tough guy said.

Daniel was surprised that anybody knew about that. After all, he'd only decided a few hour earlier. He wondered if somebody could have been spying at Mr. Miyagi's. It was possible, but he could not think of a reason why anybody would do it.

Then the younger man spoke. "My name's Mike Barnes, and I'm going to be the next All-Valley champ. See, I need your title."

"So enter the tournament and go for it," Daniel said.

"No. I need *your* title. Look, let me put it another way. You don't enter, it affects my financial future. And I'm not going to let that happen."

Daniel did not know what he was talking about, but he could understand, in a way, that a new champion would seem better if he actually beat the previous champion. Daniel had made up his mind, though. He was not going to fight.

"I don't think you have a choice," Daniel said.

The tough guys brought out an application and handed it to Daniel. Daniel didn't take it.

Mike was about to attack Daniel, but the tough guy held him back. "Let him sleep on it," he suggested to Mike. Mike looked like he wanted to make mincemeat out of Daniel right there and then, instead of waiting for the tournament. Daniel was glad the tough guy changed Mike's mind for him.

"Okay, LaRusso," Mike said. "Sleep on it. We'll see you again. Soon."

The two guys left the shop.

"Slimeball," Jessica said.

Daniel thought she was right about that, but there was something else, too. Mike Barnes reminded him of Kreese, the *sensei* from Cobra Kai. There was a hungry look in his eyes — hungry for blood.

8

The next morning in Mr. Miyagi's garden, Daniel told his partner what had happened at the shop with Mike Barnes and how he had turned down Mike's invitation to fight in the tournament.

"Proud of you, Daniel-san. Enough talk, time now to train."

Daniel was glad to return to his training. He loved studying karate with Mr. Miyagi. Even when it wasn't clear why he studied something, it always turned out to be the right thing. Mr. Miyagi was an amazing *sensei*.

Mr. Miyagi was teaching Daniel a form — or *kata*. That was a series of movements performed by one person, demonstrating many different moves, kicks, punches, blocks, and other techniques. Mr. Miyagi told Daniel that all karate is found in *kata*. Daniel thought of karate as something two people had to do together to be *real* karate, but he heard Mr. Miyagi's words.

"Now pay attention, Daniel-san. Very important lesson. Karate made of two things: *go* and *ju*. Hard and soft. Everybody thinks power of karate means hard karate. Hard block, hard punch. Real power of karate comes from learn to be soft."

That was something else that didn't make sense when Daniel first heard it. "Then how come you didn't teach me soft at first?"

"Because first must experience hard before able to understand soft. Follow me."

Mr. Miyagi began the moves of the *kata*. Daniel tried to see what was *go* and what was *ju*. He did not see much difference. Still, he did as his *sensei* had told him.

"Excuse me, Mr. Miyagi?" someone called from the gate. A middle-aged man entered. He introduced himself. "My name is Terry Silver," he said. He explained that he had just learned what Kreese had done to Mr. Miyagi at the tournament last year. He wanted to apologize for Kreese. They'd known one another since Vietnam, where Kreese had saved his life. Silver actually owned the Cobra Kai *dojo* where Kreese taught. After the tournament, when Kreese had acted so badly, all his students had quit the *dojo*. The school had closed.

"I was sent here by our karate master in Korea to apologize for John Kreese's dishonorable actions." He bowed to Mr. Miyagi.

"Accept apology," Mr. Miyagi said, bowing back.

Silver then told Daniel and Mr. Miyagi that Kreese was dead. He'd died only two weeks ago.

Daniel and Mr. Miyagi were shocked to hear that.

"After he lost his students, his heart broke. That's what he died of," Silver said. Then he turned to Daniel. "Is this your student? The champion?" He bowed to Daniel. "Our apologies to you, too," he said. There was a look of sadness on his face. Daniel even felt a little sorry about Kreese. It was sad to know that he'd been a good friend to such a nice man as Silver. Daniel wished he could have lived to change his ways.

"I'm sorry to interrupt your training," Silver said. Then he turned to go.

"Mr. Silver," Mr. Miyagi said. "Sorry to hear about death of friend."

"Me, too," Daniel added.

Silver bowed to both of them and left the garden.

Daniel began the *kata* again. His mind was on his training, but his heart felt sadness for the death of a man he had hated. Maybe, he thought, that was part of what *go* and *ju* were all about.

9

Daniel was glad Jessica was his friend. One night when he was working late, she came over to the shop with some dinner for him. It was macaroni and cheese. He just loved macaroni and cheese.

She also had something else for him. She had finished making a planter for a bonsai. It was exactly what Daniel had in mind. It was just the right size, and the color was pretty, too. Best of all, she had drawn a bonsai on the side of the pot. It was a replica of Mr. Miyagi's family crest. They were using it as a symbol for the shop.

"It's beautiful," Daniel said. Jessica was pleased that he liked it. "And I have something for you, too." He handed her two tickets. "It's for a concert at The Downstairs next month. It's this great club. Live music. I figured it would be a nice going-away present for you. It's the night before you leave."

"Hey, great! Do you like to dance?"

"You bet I do!" Daniel said.

He was about to show her his favorite dance when the door to the shop swung open, and in came Mike Barnes. This time he had two big guys with him. Daniel had hoped he'd seen the last of Mike.

"Hey, can't you read? We're closed," Daniel said.

Mike just sneered at Daniel. Then he spotted Jessica's casserole of macaroni and cheese. He made fun of it.

"Enough's enough. Get out," Daniel said.

Mike ignored Daniel's demand. "Sign the application yet?" he asked.

"Look, I told you. I'm not fighting. Now take your friends and get out."

But Mike wasn't about to leave, and he considered Daniel's statement an invitation to fight. He attacked Daniel. Daniel was so surprised that he did not have a chance to protect himself. Before he knew it, he was flying through a screen in the shop, and Mike was smashing up all the cabinets and shelves Daniel and Mr. Miyagi had worked so hard to make.

"I'm running out of patience, LaRusso," Mike said. He thrust an application and a pen into Daniel's hand. "Now sign, and let's get on with it." Daniel tore the paper in half.

Mike was about to attack again, when the door opened. It was Mr. Miyagi! The two tough guys attacked him at once. Mr. Miyagi knocked them both out at the same time!

"I'm not afraid of you, old man," Mike said.

"Mistake number one,". Mr. Miyagi said.

Mike charged at Mr. Miyagi. Mr. Miyagi stepped aside at the last second, and Mike went flying right through one of the other screens in the shop.

"Mistake number two," Mr. Miyagi said.

Mike growled and charged at Mr. Miyagi again. This time Mr. Miyagi grabbed his wrists before he could punch. He lifted Mike up by his arms, swung him around, and tossed him right out the door! The two tough guys ran through the door after him.

"Mistake number three. You're out!" Mr. Miyagi said, closing the door behind the threesome.

Daniel and Jessica laughed, because Mr. Miyagi could be very funny, especially when he was being tough. He made it look so easy!

Daniel walked Jessica back to her door. He

didn't think there would be any more trouble that night, but he didn't want her to get hurt. Then he and Mr. Miyagi cleaned up the mess. As they worked, Daniel realized that just about all of the work he and Mr. Miyagi had done had been shattered in five minutes of fighting. It made him feel sad and angry. Daniel couldn't understand why Mr. Miyagi sang cheerfully as he worked.

"How can you be singing?"

"Feel lucky."

Daniel couldn't believe his ears. "Lucky? Lucky that our whole shop just got ruined?"

"Lucky that bonsai did not. We can rebuild the shop, Daniel-san. We can't rebuild bonsai. We will sell a few of them, buy some new screens and start again."

Perhaps there *was* something to be happy about, Daniel thought. They finished up their work and drove back home together in Mr. Miyagi's truck.

But when they got home, they learned their luck had run out. All of the bonsai, which had been on a rack on Mr. Miyagi's front porch, were gone. The rack was completely empty, except for a piece of paper nailed to it.

It was an application to enter the All-Valley Tournament.

10

Daniel only saw one answer to their problem. Money. He had to get some, and the only way he knew to do that was to get Mr. Miyagi to sell the natural bonsai he'd put in Devil's Cauldron almost fifty years earlier.

He didn't want to tell Mr. Miyagi. He wanted to surprise him. It was going to mean the difference between closing the shop before it opened, and success. Daniel asked Jessica if she would help him, because she knew about mountain climbing from her clay collecting expeditions.

Jessica seemed glad to go on the expedition with Daniel and teach him how to use the ropes to lower and raise himself on the rocky face of Devil's Cauldron, but she wasn't so sure about digging up the tree.

"I still think you should have asked him before going after his tree. I mean, you think he hid it

38

on the cliff so people would go digging it up?" she asked as they walked along the trails in the woods toward Devil's Cauldron.

"Look," Daniel said. "We don't sell the tree, he loses his business. Without the business, he has no income. This tree is like money in the bank."

"Great, so now we're robbing a bank."

"Look, there's Devil's Cauldron!" Daniel said. It looked like it might once have been part of the crater of a volcano long ago. Now it was a giant cliff around a cove with almost vertical sides down to craggy rocks in the ocean. It was low tide then, so they could see the rocks as the waves broke on them. When the tide came in, the rocks would be completely submerged.

It was a beautiful place. It was frightening, too. Daniel wasn't very enthusiastic about dangling above it from a rope. But he didn't think he had a choice.

Daniel examined the cliff with his binoculars. "There!" he said.

"Can you see the tree from here?" Jessica asked.

"No, but it's the hardest place in the whole of Devil's Cauldron to reach. That has to be where Mr. Miyagi put the tree!"

Daniel was right. Working slowly and carefully,

letting out ropes to lower themselves, he and Jessica reached the slight indentation and there, just as he'd thought, was the natural bonsai.

It was incredible how the little plant had survived, clinging to the side of a cliff for almost fifty years. Daniel took out a trowel and carefully dug around the tree's roots.

"Nice and easy. I won't hurt you," he assured the plant. "From now on, regular haircuts, gourmet plant food. No more wind. No more cold."

The roots had become firmly attached to the rock. Daniel tugged to loosen them. At the same instant that the tree came loose, his rope slipped a bit, and Daniel dropped a few inches with it. The rope stopped right away and Daniel was fine, but he'd been so startled by the movement that he'd let go of the tree. It tumbled down the side of the cliff like a rag doll, and landed in a puddle of saltwater on the rocks at the bottom.

"The saltwater will kill it!" Daniel said, seeing his future slip away from him.

"Don't panic," Jessica said. "We'll go down there and get it. Follow me."

Their ropes weren't quite long enough to reach bottom. They had to unhook themselves and drop the last two feet.

They found the tree right away. Jessica took

the top off her canteen and washed the brine off the bonsai with fresh water. Daniel wrapped the roots in a plastic bag. They needed fresh dirt, moss, and clean water as quickly as possible. He wanted to hurry home.

But when they went back to their ropes, they weren't there! Someone was pulling their ropes up the cliff. They had no way out!

"Hey!" Daniel and Jessica yelled.

In answer, a piece of paper came floating down to them. It was wrapped around a pen. Daniel didn't have to unwrap it to know what it was: an application to the All-Valley Tournament.

11

"Hey, LaRusso! How are you doing?" It was Mike Barnes calling him from the top of Devil's Cauldron.

"This isn't a joke anymore!" Daniel yelled.

"It never was!" Mike yelled back.

"So let our ropes down!"

"First you sign — and if you don't, I hope you will have fun getting mashed against the rocks when the tide comes in!"

Daniel turned to Jessica. "What are our chances of getting out of here without a rope?" he asked, though he was pretty sure he knew the answer.

"None." That was what he thought.

He grabbed the paper and the pen and signed the application. As soon as Mike saw he'd signed, the ropes came tumbling down. Daniel and Jessica snapped themselves in before Mike changed his mind. Daniel got Mike and his tough guys to pull them up.

Daniel felt bad about signing the application.

"Just because you signed it doesn't mean you have to go through with it," Jessica said, trying to comfort him.

Daniel shook his head. "I don't work that way," he said. "If I say I'm going to do something, I do it."

"Even when it's blackmail?"

"It's my word," Daniel said. "And my word is good." Just then, the ropes stopped moving. They were three feet from the top of the cliff. "Hey, come on!" Daniel yelled.

"You are one heavy wimp, Daniel," one of the tough guys complained.

Then Mike stuck his head over the cliff and faced Daniel. "The application," he said, reaching out for it. Grudgingly, Daniel handed it up to him. "And don't even *think* about backing out, because then I'll be really annoyed, and you won't like me when I'm *really* annoyed."

Mike disappeared.

"Hey!" Daniel yelled. "Pull us the rest of the way! I gave you the application!"

One of the tough guys looked over the cliff at

them. "The rates just went up," he said. "I want that tree you have, too."

Daniel knew he didn't have a choice. He just hoped they wouldn't know how valuable it was. He handed the tree up to the guy.

It turned out the guy *didn't* have any idea how valuable the tree was. Instead of stealing it, he did something worse. He ripped it and stomped on it. Then Mike and his tough guys left.

Daniel and Jessica pulled themselves up over the top of the cliff. Daniel examined the tree. It was in bad shape. A lot of the needles had been torn off of it. One branch was broken. The roots were already showing damage from the saltwater. The tree lay limply in his hand. Daniel hoped Mr. Miyagi would have some magical medicine to fix it. There wasn't any time to waste.

12

Mr. Miyagi said nothing as he took the ruined tree from Daniel's hands. Daniel tried to explain. He wanted Mr. Miyagi to know why it had happened.

"I figured we could sell it so we wouldn't have to close. I didn't want it to be my fault that your dream didn't come true. I was sure the new owner would take better care of it than it could take care of itself." He thought about what he'd said. "What am I talking about? How could anybody take care of it better than how you left it?" After all, the tree had survived on a rocky cliff for fifty years all by itself!

Mr. Miyagi placed the tree in a clean pot, gently packing dirt around the drooping roots. He put moss on top of the dirt and then watered it slowly and carefully. He took the branch that was nearly broken off and reattached it with a gooey black substance.

"Is it going to be okay?" Daniel asked.

"Depend. If root strong, tree survive."

It seemed that Mr. Miyagi was talking a lot about roots these days, Daniel thought — roots of karate, roots of bonsai. Daniel wondered about his own roots.

There was a knock at the door. A delivery man pushed the door open. "Where do the bonsai trees go?" he asked.

"Leave outside."

"Trees?" Daniel asked. He walked over to the door and saw several boxes full of bonsai. "You bought these?"

"*Hai*. Sold truck."

Daniel was furious. If Mr. Miyagi had an answer to their problem, why hadn't he told Daniel and saved him all the trouble he'd just been through?

"When I woke up, you were gone," Mr. Miyagi said.

Daniel felt very dumb. Jessica was right. He *should* have asked Mr. Miyagi before digging up the tree. He could have avoided a lot of trouble, saved a natural bonsai, and not signed the application. He told Mr. Miyagi about Mike and the application at Devil's Cauldron.

"I had to make a decision on the spot and I made it."

"I understand," Mr. Miyagi said.

Daniel was surprised. "You do?" he asked.

"*Hai*, but I don't support it."

That was more like what he'd expected. He had to try, just once more, to get Mr. Miyagi's help. "I don't stand a chance against this guy unless you train me," he said.

"Understand that, too."

"Then you will train me?" Daniel asked eagerly.

"I will always train you, Daniel-san. But not for tournament. Cannot."

Daniel could train himself. He could train himself to kick, punch, and block. He could train to have endurance and strength, speed and agility. He could train himself to fight. But could he train himself to win?

13

Within the first half mile of his jog the next morning, Daniel was already breathing hard. Even Jessica was having an easier time than he was, but she wasn't worried about facing Mike Barnes at the All-Valley Tournament.

Daniel stopped and doubled over, breathing hard. "You've got to build up your wind," Jessica said.

"Why? So there will be more of it to knock out of me?" Daniel asked. He was already discouraged.

They started jogging again. Daniel promised himself he wouldn't stop until they'd gone three miles. A car honked at them. It was Terry Silver, the man who had been Kreese's friend. Daniel was glad to stop again. He introduced Silver to Jessica.

"Are you training for the Olympics or something?" Silver asked.

Daniel explained that he was getting ready for the All-Valley in a few weeks.

"Good for you. A champion should defend his title. John Kreese told me you had a lot of heart. Know how to front sweep?" he asked.

Daniel shook his head.

"Learn," Silver advised him. "Most of these tournament guys are suckers for a front sweep. You can catch them every time. You know," he added. "Since you're training by yourself, you might want to use a book I've got on sweeps. I'll drop it off at your place sometime."

Daniel thanked him. He was going to need every bit of help he could get. Books could be helpful. They weren't as good as a *sensei*, of course, but Daniel didn't have a *sensei*, so he'd make do with books.

"Nice to see you," Silver said. Daniel and Jessica waved to him.

It made Daniel feel better to know that somebody, even someone who was practically a stranger, wanted to help him. "Come on," he said to Jessica. He was ready then to run *four* miles without stopping.

After his four-mile run, Daniel continued his workout in Mr. Miyagi's garden by using a heavy bag for punching practice. It was easier to do when he had a trainer to hold the bag for him, but he didn't have that.

The gate to the garden slapped open. Mike Barnes stormed in. He was angry that Daniel had called the police and told them he'd stolen all the bonsai from the shop.

"You got no proof!" he yelled at Daniel.

"So who left the application? The tooth fairy?" Daniel asked.

Mike's short fuse blew. He attacked Daniel fiercely. Even though Daniel was ready this time, Mike seemed stronger and faster. He had Daniel in a winning clinch within seconds. In fact, Mike had Daniel around the throat and was really hurting him.

"Beat it, punk!" Daniel heard. It was Terry Silver!

Mike released Daniel and turned to attack Silver, but Silver used a front sweep technique, and Mike was on his rear end in seconds. He stood up and fled from the garden.

Silver gave Daniel a hand and helped him up. When Daniel had caught his breath, Silver gave him the book he had brought.

"Thanks," Daniel said.

"Don't mention it. But see what I mean about

sweeps?" Daniel nodded. Silver asked him who Mike was. Daniel explained as best he could. "I thought he was going to kill me," Daniel said.

"That's not what karate's about," Silver said. "It's for defense only."

"So I've been told," Daniel said. He didn't need another lesson in defense and honor. He needed lessons in karate.

Daniel asked Silver about the sweep he'd used. Silver demonstrated it and helped Daniel try the technique.

"Hey, good," Silver said, complimenting Daniel. "You know, everyone needs a teacher, Daniel. I'm opening up the Cobra Kai *dojo* again. Any time you want to train, I'm there for you. No strings attached. I mean that."

Daniel wondered. It was almost impossible to imagine training with somebody other than Mr. Miyagi. It was also almost impossible to train by himself.

Long after Silver had gone, Daniel was still trying to perfect the sweep the man had shown him. He just couldn't seem to get it right.

He wondered again about Silver's offer.

14

Mr. Miyagi's face lit into a smile when Daniel arrived at the shop. Jessica was there, too. She'd just delivered two dozen planters.

"Look, Daniel-san. Beautiful, huh?"

"I stayed up all night making them," Jessica said.

"Yeah, they're great," Daniel said quickly. His mind was on something else. "Mr. Miyagi, do you know how to sweep?" Daniel asked.

"Of course," his *sensei* answered.

"Would you mind showing me how?"

"Couldn't have asked at a better time, Daniel-san."

Mr. Miyagi stood up and walked into the back room of the shop. Daniel followed.

"I don't mean to get into anything complicated," Daniel said. "Just the basics would be great." He was really happy that Mr. Miyagi was going to help with his training. He'd been sure that in the end Mr. Miyagi wouldn't let him get beaten by Mike.

Mr. Miyagi crossed the room. There, in the corner, were all the shop's cleaning tools. Mr. Miyagi took a broom and handed it to Daniel.

"Very easy," he said. "Left hand up, right hand down. First sweep left, then right." He demonstrated his "sweeping technique." "Care to try?"

Jessica laughed. Daniel was embarrassed, and it made him angry.

"It's no joke! You don't want to show me, don't show me. Okay? But don't go making fun of me. Sorry for asking. It won't happen again!"

With that, he turned and stormed out of the store. He'd be better off with no help at all than to get help like that.

But he didn't have to get no help at all, did he? Another karate expert had offered to help him. For free. No strings attached.

Silver was working on a *kata* in front of the mirror when Daniel arrived. Daniel watched. It looked great! When he'd finished, Daniel spoke. "I, uh, gave your offer some thought."

"And?"

"And, if it's not too much trouble, I'd like to take you up on it."

"Trouble? Are you kidding? It would be an honor to teach the defending champion! When would you like to start?"

"Whenever it's convenient for you."

"How about now?" Silver asked. "There's a *gi* hanging up in the dressing room. I think it will fit you. What do you say?"

Daniel said yes.

15

The first thing Daniel learned from Silver was that he was an entirely different kind of teacher from Mr. Miyagi. Where Mr. Miyagi often taught Daniel so that he didn't always know exactly what he was learning, Silver made it perfectly clear that his purpose was to destroy the enemy.

"There are three things that make a champion. I call them the three D's: Desire, devotion, and discipline. The first two, I can't teach. The last one I can, but you have to be willing to receive it. Are you, Mr. LaRusso?"

"Yes," Daniel said.

"Yes, *sir*," Silver instructed.

"Yes, sir," Daniel said.

"That's better. Now stand up straight. I call my teaching system the Quick Silver method. I'll give you the essentials faster than any other teacher.

There are three rules and only three rules. Rule number one: A man can't stand, he can't fight. Repeat it."

He made Daniel recite the rule, almost yelling it. It was hard for Daniel to do. It wasn't that he couldn't say the words. It was just hard to change his way of thinking about karate. Still, Daniel needed a teacher and, from what he'd seen, Silver knew karate. Daniel spat the words out. Silver smiled approval.

He showed Daniel a rack that was designed to hold boards of wood at the three critical levels of a person, the ankles and knees, the chest, and the head. There was a thick board at the lowest point, representing a man's lower leg.

"Sweep it," Terry told Daniel.

Daniel tried the sweeping technique Silver had showed him earlier that day. It had worked against Mike Barnes, but when Daniel used it against the board, he just hit his foot.

"Higher!" Silver told him.

Daniel knew that if he hit it higher, he'd be aiming for his opponent's knees, and that could be dangerous. It was also completely illegal in a tournament bout. Daniel started to tell Silver that, but he cut him off.

"Did you come here to teach or to be taught?"

Daniel hit the board higher. It hurt his foot.

"Harder!"

"Ouch!"

"Ouch is not a word we use here, Mr. LaRusso," Silver said. "Now try again."

"Isn't this a little extreme?" Daniel asked, looking at his foot, which was turning red. "Sir?" he added.

Silver began his answer with a *kiaiiiii!* He swept at the board and smashed it to pieces. "Extreme situations require extreme measures. Come back in the morning," he said, dismissing Daniel. "You did good for the first day."

Silver turned and left the *dojo*, returning to his office in the back. Daniel limped to the dressing room, changed his clothes, and walked out to his car. If that was good, Daniel wondered if he'd be able to walk when he did *very* good!

He hoped Mr. Miyagi wouldn't see him come home. Daniel was ashamed of his sore foot and didn't want his friend to see it. He went straight to his room.

Almost immediately, there was a knock at the door. Mr. Miyagi came in, carrying a bucket of water and a bag of something.

"Daniel-san, what happened to foot?"

"Oh, I must have banged it on something and

I didn't notice," Daniel lied. He knew he wasn't fooling Mr. Miyagi, but the old man didn't say anything. He just poured some powder out of the bag into the bucket.

"Soak foot in that. By tomorrow you'll be fine."

"Why? What's in there? A new foot for me?" Daniel joked.

"No, next best thing. New foot powder."

Daniel sniffed. It smelled awful. "What's in there?" he asked.

"Better you don't know. Here." He put Daniel's foot in the bucket. Daniel thought he could feel the healing power right away.

"I don't know what I'd do without you," he said.

"Probably spend a lot more time in doctor's office," Mr. Miyagi said. "Good night, Daniel-san."

"Good night," Daniel said. Mr. Miyagi left the room.

Daniel lay back in his bed, dangling his foot in the warm water. He felt all mixed-up inside. Mr. Miyagi was his friend. He took care of him when he was hurt, but Daniel was studying karate with someone else.

Once again, he wished Mr. Miyagi would give in, but Daniel knew that he would not.

16

The next day, Daniel returned to the Cobra Kai *dojo* for his second lesson.

"Rule number two: A man can't breathe, he can't fight," Silver said. He walked over to a punching bag like the one Daniel had been working with at Mr. Miyagi's. Daniel stood on the far side of the bag and held it steady for him. "Now imagine this is the enemy," Silver said. "These are his ribs right here." He gestured toward the bag. "Behind his ribs, his lungs." Silver lunged at the bag and struck it very hard. He almost knocked Daniel over! "Now you try," he said.

Daniel didn't like the idea of it. He'd never thought of the person he was sparring with as his enemy. It was an opponent. Then he thought of Mike Barnes. Maybe *he* really was an enemy, not just an opponent.

Daniel flexed his knees and got into position to strike. Before he could try it, though, Silver stopped him and took him over to the rack that held a thick board. Today the board was at chest level. "Right here," he said, pointing to the center of the board. "Lay into it."

Swiftly, Daniel struck out at the board. He hit it so hard with the back of his arm that he wrenched his elbow. "Ow!" He rubbed his elbow. "Why do we have to do this?" he asked.

There was a fierce look in Silver's eyes when he answered Daniel's question. "Because you don't go hunting elephants with peashooters. And until you learn what I'm teaching you, all you've got is a peashooter!"

"I did okay last time," Daniel reminded him.

Silver sneered. "Last time, you weren't fighting this!" he said. Then he swiveled the wooden board at head level on the rack. It had a picture of Mike Barnes on it. Just looking at Mike Barnes made Daniel angry enough to hit the wood.

He slammed away at it.

When he was finished with his practice, he still hadn't broken the wood, but he'd done an awfully good job on his arm and his elbow. They were red and swollen and very sore. Daniel hoped the magic foot powder would be magic arm powder as well.

That night, he mixed the potion and stuck his arm in the bucket. Mr. Miyagi knocked and came into his room. Daniel didn't want him to see what had happened, but there was no way to hide it.

"Daniel-san, why you do this to yourself?" he asked.

Daniel wasn't sure he knew the answer, but he did know how Silver would answer the question. "Because extreme situations require extreme measures," he said.

Mr. Miyagi looked a little sad for Daniel. It made Daniel angry. "Look, I've got problems," Daniel reminded him. "And if you're not going to be part of the solution, don't give me a hard time about it, okay?"

Mr. Miyagi left Daniel by himself. He soaked his arm for an hour. He was very relieved to see that the powder did work again and that the pain was gone. Mr. Miyagi was asleep when Daniel returned the powder to the cabinet in his room. As he left the room, he noticed the natural bonsai. Mr. Miyagi was keeping it on his bedside table so he could watch it carefully. It needed a lot of watching. It was in worse shape than it had been when Daniel had brought it home. All of its needles were gone and the broken branch sagged pathetically.

It looks like I feel, Daniel thought, and the thought didn't comfort him at all.

17

Silver was busy in the office when Daniel arrived for his next lesson. He changed into a *gi*, went into the *dojo*, and began working by himself, practicing the *kata* Mr. Miyagi had been teaching him.

He was feeling cheerful. For one thing, he enjoyed the *kata*. It was a way for him to perfect his movements in each technique. That was fun. Another thing that made him cheerful was that he and Jessica were going to the rock concert that night. He was meeting her outside the place at nine o'clock. That was something he could really look forward to.

"What are you wasting your time with a *kata* for? Didn't I tell you it is useless in the tournament?" Silver was standing by the door to his office with his hands on his hips. He seemed really annoyed with Daniel. Daniel stopped doing the *kata* and listened carefully.

"Rule number three: A man can't see, he can't fight. Hit him square in the nose. He'll be blinded by tears, probably break his nose, and then he'll be choking on his own blood. Make a fist."

Daniel didn't even bother to remind Silver that hits to the head didn't count in a tournament. In fact, if the referee thought you did it on purpose, it could cost a point. He'd learned that Silver's karate wasn't always just exactly what was in the usual rule book. He did what Silver told him and made a fist.

"Good. Now here's what you do. You wait until your man is moving forward, and when he's close in so the action's confused, take him and . . . *kiaiii!*" He slashed at the top board on the rack. The wood broke in two easily. "He runs into your fist, see? Not your fault. He can't continue. You win. Now you try it." He put a fresh board on the rack for Daniel.

Daniel tried it. It hurt. "Do it again!" Silver commanded.

Daniel punched again, more sharply this time. "Ow!"

"Mr. LaRusso, you're not concentrating."

Maybe that was true. Maybe he just needed to

focus everything on the board. He'd done that before. Once in Okinawa he'd slashed through slabs of ice. If he could do that, he could break wood. He concentrated.

He kept hitting away at the wood, harder and harder. He started thinking that the wooden boards on the rack in front of him were Mike Barnes.

Daniel could practically see him. Mike Barnes making fun of Jessica's food, Mike Barnes pulling up the ropes by Devil's Cauldron, Mike Barnes busting up all the furniture in the shop, Mike Barnes attacking him in Mr. Miyagi's garden. Suddenly, Daniel felt transformed. He felt as if he were a karate machine. He charged at the rack. "*Kiaiiiiii!*" First he swept at the low board with his ankle. It snapped in two. Then he slashed the middle board with his arm. It shattered. Finally, he punched the board at head level. His fist went right through it!

"All right!" Silver said. "You're ready!"

"I am ready!" Daniel said and he was absolutely sure it was true. Even Mike Barnes couldn't withstand punishment like that.

18

The first thing Daniel saw when he pulled his car up in front of the bonsai shop was a sign that read HELP WANTED. The shop had been open for a few days and business was going pretty well — well enough for Mr. Miyagi to get his truck back, but Daniel didn't think they were ready to start hiring other people. He picked up the sign from the front window and carried it over to the cash register. Mr. Miyagi had just finished ringing up a sale.

"What do we need help for?" he asked Mr. Miyagi.

"We don't. I do. The shop is too much for one person to run."

"But I'm here," Daniel said.

"Where?" Mr. Miyagi asked. "This is only the second time in a week and it's already four-thirty."

Daniel felt guilty, because Mr. Miyagi was

right. He wanted to make it up to him. "Okay, tomorrow I'm here," he promised. "Eight o'clock sharp, on the button, to open up."

"Tomorrow is Sunday, Daniel-san. We are closed."

"So you're firing me?"

"That's not what I'm saying."

"Well, it sure sounds like it, and it sure looks like it." He waved the sign in Mr. Miyagi's face.

"Then maybe you should get eyes and ears checked if that's what you're hearing and seeing."

"There's nothing wrong with my eyes and ears!"

"Then maybe there's something wrong with your training, Daniel-san, that sends you home bruised and bloodied and angry, and makes you forget your other responsibilities."

That made Daniel so angry he was practically seeing red. "That's what this is all about, isn't it? You thought I would quit the tournament because I couldn't do it without you. But now that you see that I am, and I *can*, you're using the shop to blackmail me! Well, it's not going to work. You can keep the whole shop. I don't care!"

Daniel stormed out of the shop, slamming the door behind him. He threw the HELP WANTED sign in the gutter.

19

Daniel waved to Jessica. She was waiting for him outside the rock-and-roll club.

"I didn't know if you would be here," she said. "I heard about the Help Wanted sign."

"I want to explain about that," Daniel said. He told her that he'd been under a lot of pressure but that he was working things out. "Things are coming together for me now. My training's great, and I'll be okay."

"Well then, let's go rock and roll!" Jessica said.

They went into the club. It was dark and noisy. The music was great. They started dancing right away and didn't stop until they were so thirsty they just had to get a soda. He led the way over to the soda bar and got onto the end of the line. While they waited Daniel looked around. He was surprised to see his *sensei*, Terry Silver, there.

"Hi," Silver said. "Let me buy you something to drink."

They were waiting in the line and talking about the music when a guy about Daniel's age started talking to Jessica.

"I've been watching you dance," he said. "You're really pretty. My name's Rudy."

Jessica seemed uncomfortable, and Daniel didn't like the way the boy was talking to her.

"She's with me," Daniel said.

"Says who?" the guy asked.

"I am," Jessica told him. Daniel put his arm around her as if to protect her.

Rudy slapped Daniel on the shoulder. "Hey!" Rudy said.

Daniel didn't even think. In an instant, he whirled around and slammed his fist into Rudy's face. Rudy fell backwards through the crowd. He put his hands up to his face and yelled so everybody in the place could hear it. "He broke my nose! He broke my nose!"

Someone screamed. The crowd started yelling "Fight! Fight!"

Daniel looked at his hand. He was stunned. He could hardly believe what he had done. And the worst part was that it had been easy!

Jessica looked at him in horror. "What's wrong

with you?" she asked. Before Daniel had a chance to think or to answer, she turned and ran out of the club.

Daniel was going to follow her, but he saw the guards rushing toward him. Silver tapped him on the shoulder. "Come on!" he said. He led Daniel past the back of the soda bar, through the kitchen, and out the back door. They didn't stop running until they were in the parking lot.

Daniel leaned up against a car. He was breathing hard. It wasn't running that had winded him. Daniel didn't know what it was. He was upset.

Silver spoke excitedly. "Did you see how it worked, Daniel? You didn't even think. Something got in your way. Bang! Down it went! Technique and killer instinct. You've got it all now, kid. You're ready!"

Daniel looked at him. In Silver, Daniel saw himself and what he'd just done, and he understood why Jessica had run away from him. He'd just done the cruelest thing he'd ever done to anybody, and his *sensei* was giving him an A+ for it!

He wanted to run just the same way Jessica had — only he wanted to run away from himself.

"I've got to go!" Daniel said.

"What's the matter?" Silver asked. "Where are you going?"

"I've just got to get out of here!" He left Silver standing in the parking lot. He wasn't sure what he was going to do, but he knew one thing for sure — he was done with the Quick Silver method. For good.

20

Daniel's first stop was at Jessica's. He knew she was leaving the next day. They'd probably never see one another again, but he couldn't let her go without saying he was sorry.

"What do you want?" she asked.

"Can I talk to you?"

"I'm busy," she said.

Daniel thought he deserved that. He wasn't surprised she didn't want to see him. "It'll only take a minute," he said.

She let him in.

"I want to apologize for what I did. It shouldn't have happened."

"Tell that to the guy whose nose you broke."

"I'm going to," Daniel promised. "I wanted you to know, though, that it wasn't me."

"I know," she said. "It was Conan the Barbarian!"

Daniel smiled at her joke. Jessica smiled a little bit, too. He explained that he'd realized after he'd punched Rudy that everything he'd been learning was leading up to that. "I feel like I'm losing control," he said. "And I'm losing my best friend, Mr. Miyagi, and my newest friend, you."

"Just because I got upset doesn't mean we're not friends," Jessica said. "And Mr. Miyagi's your friend, too. He has faith in you. He loves you."

"Wait until he hears what I did."

"Well, I think he'd better hear it from you first," she said. Daniel knew she was right about that. The worst thing would be if he heard it from somebody else.

"I guess you're right," Daniel said. "Thanks. And thanks for still being a friend."

"You're welcome."

Daniel felt better. He was glad Jessica wasn't angry with him anymore. And he was glad she'd told him Mr. Miyagi had faith in him. He just hoped he could make up with Mr. Miyagi as easily as he had with Jessica.

He had to hurry back home then. He said good night and good-bye to Jessica. They promised to write to each other and keep in touch.

*   *   *

As soon as Daniel got home, he called the local hospital to see if Rudy was all right. They hadn't had anybody come in with a broken nose. That seemed strange to Daniel. Maybe he hadn't broken his nose after all. Daniel wanted to apologize to Rudy, but if he couldn't find him, he couldn't apologize. And in the meantime, he needed to apologize to somebody else.

Daniel found Mr. Miyagi in his garden, sitting quietly in the cool evening darkness. Daniel sat down next to him. He thought about all the things that had been happening. His thoughts made him feel awful and ashamed. Then he started to cry. Mr. Miyagi waited until Daniel was ready to talk.

"I've been so angry at you for not teaching me I didn't stop to think what I was learning. It was all wrong. Now I feel dead inside. I feel like that tree that I killed — all broken and twisted. I'm just pulled apart. That guy, Terry Silver, was training me for the tournament, but I got all messed up. I feel I hurt you and me and it's never going to heal."

Mr. Miyagi was quiet for a while until Daniel had stopped crying. "Miyagi show you something," he said.

He stood up and walked through the house.

Daniel followed him. There, on the front porch, in the bonsai rack, was the natural bonsai. It was better! The broken branch was still alive, and the tree was even growing new needles. Daniel could barely believe it.

"Everything can heal," Mr. Miyagi said. "It just takes time. And care."

"And strong roots?" Daniel asked. Mr. Miyagi told him it was true. Then the two friends bowed to each other. It felt wonderful to Daniel.

"Boy, it's been lonely without you," Daniel said.

"Been lonely without you, too."

"Well, I'm back now. For good. I just have to go tell Silver I'm dropping out. I won't be long."

Daniel didn't want to wait until the morning to tell Silver. He didn't think he'd sleep until it was done. He pulled out his car keys and walked down the steps to the driveway.

"Want Miyagi go with you?" his friend offered.

"I got myself in, I'll get myself out. Thanks for being here," Daniel said.

"Where else would I be?" Mr. Miyagi asked.

21

Although it was very late, there was a light on in the office at the Cobra Kai *dojo*. Daniel opened the door and walked in. He could hear noises from the office.

"Mr. Silver?"

Silver came out of the office. "There you are. Where did you go?"

For some reason, Daniel felt nervous. "I, uh, had to think about things, Mr. Silver. I've decided not to defend the title. I appreciate what you were trying to do for me, so I wanted to let you know my decision in person."

Silver looked very angry. "You owe me something, Danny boy!"

Daniel promised to pay for the lessons he'd had.

"I don't want payment in money," Silver said.

"The way you're going to pay me is to defend your title!"

Daniel was surprised. He hadn't realized Silver cared so much about that. "You can't make me do something I don't want to do."

Silver just smiled. "I've been making you do things you didn't want to all along!" He laughed. "Now I'll show you what I mean. Come on over here!" Silver called toward his office.

Somebody else walked out of Silver's office then.

It was Mike Barnes.

That could only mean one thing: Silver was the one who was paying Mike to win Daniel's title from him! So everything Silver had taught Daniel was to get him to lose to Mike!

"This is all business, you understand, Daniel," Silver said.

"You guys are crazy! You're not going to pull this off. And there's no way I'm going to be part of your scheme!"

Daniel turned to run out of the *dojo*. He didn't want to stay there one second longer. When he got to the door, there was a very big man blocking the exit — and that man was John Kreese. He was very much alive! Daniel realized then that everything Silver had said to him and to Mr. Miyagi was a lie. All Silver wanted was to make Daniel look bad at the tournament. And he would do anything to accomplish that.

Kreese laughed when he saw the look on Daniel's face.

Then Mike attacked Daniel. Mike was a dirty fighter. He'd learned everything the Quick Silver method had to offer — and then some. Daniel tried to fight back, but too much was happening too fast. He couldn't concentrate. Things were looking bad for him.

Until help arrived. It was Mr. Miyagi!

First Mr. Miyagi took care of Mike without ever laying a hand on him. Mike charged at Mr. Miyagi. Mr. Miyagi stepped aside at the last possible second. Mike rammed into the wall, headfirst. He was out cold!

Then Kreese tried *his* luck. He was no better against Miyagi this time than he had been in the parking lot after Daniel's championship bout the year before. Silver tried to fight Mr. Miyagi, too, but it was no good. Silver ended up sitting on the floor next to Kreese, scratching his head. He couldn't figure out what he'd done wrong.

Daniel and Mr. Miyagi walked toward the door.

Silver spoke to them from where he sat on the floor.

"You think this is the end of it? After my boy wins the title, I'm going to open Cobra Kai *dojos* all over this valley. I might even give lessons for free! From now on, when people say karate around here, the only thing they'll mean is Cobra Kai karate. John Kreese's karate. You won't even be a memory!"

That was it. He was in this for the money! Silver had figured that if his champion beat Daniel, it would really mean a lot. The fact was that if his champion won, no matter *who* he beat, it would be good for Silver's reputation. It would mean the Cobra Kai method was the best. It would mean that hundreds of youngsters would learn to kick knees and break noses. Daniel couldn't let that happen!

He turned to Mr. Miyagi. "*Now* will you train me?" Daniel asked.

"*Hai*, Daniel-san. Now I will train you."

They left Cobra Kai. There was a lot of work to be done, and little time to do it. The tournament was in only two weeks!

22

G o and *ju*. Hard and soft. Daniel studied these
things carefully. He worked on his *kata* for
hours at a time until he could do it in his sleep.
Mr. Miyagi worked with him every second. Daniel
learned new techniques of soft karate, how to
kick, duck, block, and punch.

Daniel knew that, on the other side of town,
Mike was smashing wood and turning bricks into
powder. Maybe that worked for some people. It
didn't work for Daniel.

He practiced his ducks. He spent time medi-
tating with Mr. Miyagi. They worked hard on
Daniel's training.

Then on a Sunday, when the shop was closed,
they went on a very important trip together. They
returned the natural bonsai to its home on the cliff
of Devil's Cauldron. They hung from ropes fas-
tened at the top of the Cauldron just as Daniel

had done with Jessica. Mr. Miyagi dug a fresh hole for the tree. He replanted it.

Daniel was happy to see the tree back where it belonged. The broken branch was doing fine, and there were fresh green needles all over it. It was hard to believe it was the same tree, but it was.

"Tree has strong root now. So do you, Daniel-san," Mr. Miyagi told him as he patted the earth around the tree's roots. "And like tree chooses how it grows, so you, too, can now choose how you grow. Take what you learn and make it work for you."

"I feel like I don't know anything," Daniel said.

"That is always first step to knowing something. I have faith in you."

Mr. Miyagi began inching up the cliff. Daniel waited for a second. He looked at the tree. He was sure it would be fine now. He hated to think what had almost happened to it because of him. "Sorry," he said to the tree.

A breeze brushed the branches of the bonsai then. They moved gently in the wind. Daniel thought they almost looked like they were saying good-bye to him. He knew it would be okay. It could take care of itself.

23

Daniel and Mr. Miyagi entered the tournament arena just in time to hear the announcer tell the audience that Terry Silver was opening a whole chain of Cobra Kai *dojos*. The audience clapped and cheered. A lot of them were wearing the free Cobra Kai T-shirts that were being handed out. Daniel turned one down when it was offered to him.

They watched Mike win his semifinal match. It made Daniel sick to see how Mike beat his opponent — as if he were really an *enemy*, not just a high school kid. The sight made Daniel more determined than ever. He had to win and beat Cobra Kai for good.

Karate was a sport. It was fun, and it had helped Daniel learn a lot about life. It could be used to defend honor or for protection. Those were the good things about it. Some people, Daniel had learned, used it for the wrong reasons. They used it to attack, to hurt, to destroy. That wasn't what karate was for. Daniel understood that this match with Mike was more than a match between two karate students. It was a match that would determine what kind of karate would be taught and learned in the Valley for a long time to come.

Daniel had to win.

Mike Barnes was tough. Daniel knew that. He just had to be tougher!

It was time for their match. The referee introduced them. He reminded them that a point was scored if they made contact with the front of their opponent's body, above the waist. Anything else didn't count. The match would last three minutes. The first one to get three points would win. Then he told them to bow. Every karate match began and ended with a bow. Daniel bowed. Mike did not. He just glared at Daniel. The referee told Mike again to bow. Grudgingly, he nodded his head at Daniel.

Mike scored right away. Daniel couldn't believe how fierce he was. He charged like an angry rhino! There was no way to block the blows!

Mike attacked again, but this time he hit Daniel

below the waist and lost a point. Daniel could see that Mike's face was red with fury. It was frightening.

Mike charged again. Daniel tried to block the kick, but while he did that, Mike attacked his ribs. It hurt!

Mike won a point, but lost it when he tried another illegal punch and the referee caught him. Then the buzzer sounded. The referee called a time-out.

"I can't beat him, Mr. Miyagi," Daniel told his teacher.

"You must beat him," the *sensei* said. Daniel knew he was right. If Mike won, Cobra Kai *dojos* would be opening up all over the place, like fast-food restaurants. Only they would be Quick Silver punching schools.

"You've got to give me a secret technique!" Daniel said.

"Everything you need, Daniel-san, you have. Remember lesson of natural bonsai. Tree with strong root chooses own way to grow. Like tree, you have strong root. Follow own way. Remember *go* and *ju*. Hard, soft. And remember, Daniel-san, all karate is found in *kata*."

Go, *ju*, and *kata*. Daniel thought about these

things in the short seconds until the match resumed.

Then it all made sense to Daniel. Mike only knew one kind of karate — hard karate. Daniel could beat him with his knowledge. He could win by being soft!

The referee called for the match to start again. The score was tied at zero to zero. Because the buzzer had already sounded, the match was now in "sudden death" overtime. That meant that the first person to score a point would be the winner.

Mike lunged at Daniel. Daniel stepped aside. Mike flew past him and out of the ring. The crowd laughed. Mike charged again. Daniel rolled out of his way and bounced back up to his feet.

"I'm going to kill you!" Mike hissed at Daniel.

That was just what Daniel wanted to hear. The angrier Mike got, the harder he'd fight, and the easier it would be to beat him by being soft!

Daniel began doing his *kata* — the root of all karate, as Mr. Miyagi had said. He knew the movements so well that he almost didn't have to think.

Mike had to think a lot, though. He was very confused by Daniel's display. He tried to punch and kick, but no matter how he attacked, when he got there, Daniel wasn't there. Daniel's moves were so smooth and so quick that Mike couldn't lay a hand on him!

Mike lunged a final time. Daniel shifted his weight and moved a fraction of an inch. Mike's punch landed on thin air. Daniel spun around and delivered a side hammer blow right to his target.

Mike didn't even know what hit him, but everybody else did.

"Point! LaRusso! Winner!" The referee announced.

He'd done it! He'd won! He was champion again, but it wasn't his own victory that made him happy this time. This time he was happy because he knew that what had really won was Mr. Miyagi's karate. Cobra Kai was gone for good!